Ralph's Rules for Feelings

Talar Herculian Coursey & Riley Herculian Coursey

Illustrated by Meri Andreasyan

Ralphy's Rules for Feelings

Ralphy's Rules for Feelings with Furrapist, Jackson Johnson
Copyright © 2023 by Talar Herculian Coursey
All rights reserved. No part of this book may be used or reproduced in any manner without written permission from the publisher, except as provided by the United States of America copyright law or brief quotations embodied in articles and reviews.

The scanning, uploading, and distribution of this book via the Internet or via any other means without the permission of the publisher is illegal and punishable by law.
Illustrations by Meri Andreasyan
Formatting by Sunny Duran
Published by Purple Butterfly Press
www.purplebutterflypress.net

ISBN (hardcover): 978-1-955119-45-0
ISBN (paperback): 978-1-955119-46-7
ISBN (ebook): 978-1-955119-47-4
Library of Congress Control Number: 2023906182
Printed in the United States of America

Publisher's Cataloging-in-Publication Data

Names: Coursey, Talar Herculian, author. | Coursey, Riley Herculian, author. | Andreasyan, Meri, illustrator.
Title: Ralphy's rules for feelings : with furrapist, Jackson Johnson / Talar Herculian Coursey & Riley Herculian Coursey ; illustrated by Meri Andreasyan.
Description: Columbia, SC : Purple Butterfly Press, 2023. | Includes 36 pages of color illustrations. | Series: Ralphy's rules ; 2. | Audience: Ages 3-8. | Summary: Ralphy is a happy dog who teaches emotional regulation and intelligence to young readers using the example of going to school.
Identifiers: LCCN 2023906182 | ISBN 9781955119450 (hardback) | ISBN 9781955119467 (pbk.) | ISBN 9781955119474 (ebook)
Subjects: LCSH: Dogs -- Juvenile fiction. | Emotional intelligence -- Juvenile fiction. | School children -- Juvenile literature. | School environment -- Juvenile literature. | BISAC: JUVENILE FICTION / Animals / Dogs. | JUVENILE FICTION / Social Themes / Emotions & Feelings. | JUVENILE FICTION / School & Education.
Classification: LCC PZ7.1 C68 Ral 2023 | DDC [E]--dc22
LC record available at https://lccn.loc.gov/ 2023906182

Ralphy's Rules for Feelings

Talar Herculian Coursey & Riley Herculian Coursey

Illustrated by Meri Andreasyan

**In memory of
Shane McCallan, Co-Founder of ComplyAuto**

**Meet Ralphy. Ralphy is a dog.
Ralphy is a happy dog.**

Today, Ralphy is driving the school bus.

And Jackson Johnson is riding next to him.
Jackson Johnson is a Furrapist.
He helps kids understand their feelings.
Ralphy has brought Jackson Johnson to help the kids
going to school learn Ralphy's Rules about feelings.

Jaseena gets on the bus.

"Good morning! How are you today?" asks Jackson Johnson.

"I'm **scared** about how my first day of school will go," says Jaseena. "What if I don't like my teacher? Or what if my teacher doesn't like me?"

"It's ok to be scared," says Jackson Johnson. "Everybody is scared sometimes. But, even if you're scared, you can still be **brave** and try new things. Bring scared with you and put it on the seat. When you get off the bus to go to school, you can take scared with you or you can leave it on the seat."

LaKeisha gets on the bus.

"Good morning! How are you today?" asks Jackson Johnson.

"I'm *sad* to leave my mom," says LaKeisha.

"It's ok to be sad. It's ok to miss your mom," says Jackson Johnson. "She misses you, too, but she'll be so *happy* to see you when you come home from school. Bring sad with you and put it on the seat. When you get off the bus to go to school, you can take sad with you or you can leave it on the seat."

Riley gets on the bus.

"Good morning! How are you today?" asks Jackson Johnson.

"I'm **tired**," says Riley. "I had to get up early for school."

"It's ok to feel tired," says Jackson Johnson. "Make sure you drink lots of water and eat healthy snacks. Bring tired with you and put it on the seat. When you get off the bus, you can take tired with you or you can leave it on the seat."

Cairo gets on the bus.

"Good morning! How are you today?" asks Jackson Johnson.

"I'm **nervous** about meeting new people," says Cairo.

"It's ok to be nervous," says Jackson Johnson. "Lots of kids are nervous today. Bring nervous with you and put it on the seat. When you get off the bus, you can take nervous with you or you can leave it on the seat."

Jude gets on the bus.

"Good morning! How are you today?" asks Jackson Johnson.

"I'm **embarrassed** to get on the bus and not know where to sit," says Jude.

"It's ok to feel embarrassed. You can sit wherever your legs take you," says Jackson Johnson. "Bring embarrassed with you and put it on the seat. When you get off the bus, you can take embarrassed with you or you can leave it on the seat."

Indie gets on the bus.

"Good morning! How are you today?" asks Jackson Johnson.

"I'm **excited**!" says Indie.

"Great," says Jackson Johnson. "Bring excited with you and put excited on the seat next to you. When you get off the bus, you can take excited with you or you can leave it on the seat."

The children sat on the bus with scared, sad, tired, nervous, embarrassed, and excited sitting beside them.

"You have all brought your feelings with you today and they are all welcome on our bus," says Jackson Johnson. "You get to decide whether you want to keep your feelings with you when you get off the bus or if you want to leave them on your seat."

"But how do we do that?" asks LaKeisha. "How do I decide not to be sad?"

"That is a great question," says Jackson Johnson. "You decide not to be sad by changing what you think."

"What are you thinking that makes you feel sad?" asks Jackson Johnson.

"I'm thinking that I miss my mom," says LaKeisha

"That's good," says Jackson Johnson. "You did a good job explaining what you're thinking.

"There's nothing wrong with what you're thinking. But, if your thinking makes you feel sad and you don't want to feel sad, what is another thought you could be thinking that would make you feel not sad?"

Hmmmm, thinks LaKeisha.

"I guess I could think about how much I like playing jump rope with my friends at school. If I think about that, it makes me not feel sad."

"Good job," says Jackson Johnson. "Give it a try. Picture yourself playing with your friends."

LaKeisha pictures herself playing with friends.

"How do you feel now?" asks Jackson Johnson.

"I feel **happy**!" says LaKeisha.

"So, you see, you get to decide whether you want to keep feeling the feelings you brought on the bus or if you want to feel something else," says Jackson Johnson.

"I want to try it," says Jude.

"Ok, Jude. Let's give it a try," says Jackson Johnson. "What is the thought you're thinking that makes you feel embarrassed?"

"I'm thinking that if I sit next to someone, they might laugh at me or give me a dirty look."

"What is a thought you can think that would help you not to feel embarrassed?" asks Jackson Johnson.

"I don't know," says Jude.

"What if you did know? What would be your thought?" asks Jackson Johnson.

"I guess if I thought about my Superman shirt and how Superman is so strong, I would feel strong and not feel embarrassed," says Jude.

"That's a great thought! Give it a try." says Jackson Johnson.

"How does that feel?" asks Jackson Johnson.

Smiling, Jude says, "I don't feel so embarrassed anymore. I feel **strong**!"

"Well done!" Jackson Johnson says.

One by one, the children get off the bus and leave **scared, tired, sad, embarrassed,** and **nervous** on the bus.

Indie decides that she wants to keep excited and take it to school.

Whenever you have a feeling, remember that—

It's ok to feel your feelings.

You get to decide if you want to keep feeling that way or change it.

If you want to change how you feel, change what you're thinking.

Now you try it.

What are you feeling?

The End

For Real.

Seriously, nothing more.
©Talar Herculian Coursey, 2023

Talar Herculian Coursey is a lawyer by day (General Counsel for ComplyAuto) and a children's book author, Life Coach and philanthropist by night (more like mornings). Her first children's book, Ralphy's Rules for Living the Good Life, was first published in 2021. A new edition was published in 2023 by Purple Butterfly Press.

Connect with Talar on her website. www.TalarEsq.com

Meri Andreasyan lives and creates in Yerevan, Armenia. She graduated from the Academy of Fine Arts as a printmaker.

Her works were shown in different printmaking exhibitions, won awards, and were even published in famous foreign art magazines. Besides printmaking, she loves illustrating for children's books.

Meri leads a healthy lifestyle. She enjoys hiking, and Armenia is a great destination for it, as every step you take is a mountain to climb. Every morning starts with yoga, and after, the whole day passes in a good, quiet, productive, and creative manner.

andreasyanmeri99@gmail.com

AFTERWORD

A few years ago, I had the distinct pleasure of introducing a bright, inspired, and incredibly charitable woman to these life-altering coaching concepts. And like me, she reached the unavoidable conclusion that we should be teaching "this stuff" to people much sooner, when they are younger, so they can spend their whole lives implementing these teachings instead of struggling to do it the old, unsustainable way. "We have to tell the kids," she said to me. And then she set out to do exactly that.

Through her Ralphy's Rules series, Talar has made it her mission to teach these vital life skills to children, so they are better equipped to face life as it comes at them in real time, as opposed to watching them struggle for years and years before sharing with them these unwavering truths. She understands that the sooner people learn of these concepts, the better the world collectively becomes. She has an art for distilling complex coaching concepts and making these foundational principles approachable even to the littlest learners. Through her whimsical and inventive storytelling, she makes it possible for our youngest generation to easily digest lessons that will serve them today, tomorrow, and every other day of their incredibly bright futures.

-Olivia Vizachero, *The Less Stressed Lawyer, Certified Master Coach*

Read more about this book here: https://talaresq.com/afterword/